PUFFIN BOOKS
GAUTAMA BUDDHA

Sonia Mehta is a children's writer who believes that sparking off a child's imagination opens up a world of adventure. She has been writing for children for over two decades. Her body of work is wide-ranging—she created one of India's first dedicated children's newspaper sections; conceptualized the *Cadbury Bournvita Quiz Contest* for TV; and has written books, songs, poems and stories for leading publishers in India, several African nations, the USA and the UK.

She lives in Mumbai and runs Quadrum Solutions, a content company she co-founded. She is also the co-founder of PodSquad, a retail children's edutainment brand that firmly believes that children learn best when they are having fun.

Most days, Sonia can be found pounding away at her computer—when she is not playing with her dachshunds, the two little loves of her life.

Read More in the Junior Lives Series

Mother Teresa
Mahatma Gandhi
Rani Lakshmibai

Gautama Buddha

Sonia Mehta

Illustrated by Jitendra Mahadik

PUFFIN BOOKS

An imprint of Penguin Random House

PUFFIN BOOKS

USA | Canada | UK | Ireland | Australia
New Zealand | India | South Africa | China | Singapore

Puffin Books is part of the Penguin Random House group of companies
whose addresses can be found at global.penguinrandomhouse.com

Published by Penguin Random House India Pvt Ltd
4th Floor, Capital Tower 1, MG Road,
Gurugram 122 002, Haryana, India

First published in Puffin Books by Penguin Random House India 2018

Text and illustrations copyright © Quadrum Solutions Pvt. Ltd 2018
Series copyright © Penguin Random House India 2018

ISBN 9780143428244

Design and layout by Quadrum Solutions Pvt. Ltd
Printed at Repro India Limited

www.penguin.co.in

This is a legitimate digitally printed version of the book and therefore might not
have certain extra finishing on the cover.

Contents

1 It's a Boy!

Queen Mahamaya was going to have a baby. There was great excitement all around the kingdom.

'My lord,' the queen said to her husband, King Shudhodhana, who was the king of the Sakya kingdom, 'it is time for me to go to my parents' house for the birth of our baby.' It was the custom in those days for women to bear their babies at their parents' home. The king made arrangements immediately, and the queen was on her way.

Sakya was a small tribal kingdom, in what is present-day Nepal. And it was a

Did You Know?

Part of the Kosala Empire, the kingdom of Sakya was situated on the banks of the River Ganga, close to the Himalayan foothills. Kapilavastu was its capital. The locals practised a religion called Sanatana dharma, which later became the basis of Hinduism.

long journey to the queen's parents' home in the Koliya kingdom. The queen was carried in a royal palanquin, with guards walking alongside. Soon they crossed some beautiful gardens in a place called Lumbini. The sun was blazing down and the queen wanted to rest.

'Let us rest here awhile,' the queen ordered the palanquin-bearers. They stopped at once, and the queen settled down under the shade of a sal tree. Suddenly, she felt a sharp pain.

'The baby is coming!' she cried out to the midwife. And sure enough, under a bright, blue sky, surrounded by lovely trees, her baby boy was born. That little baby grew up to become one of the world's most influential religious leaders— Gautama Buddha.

Oh Really?

According to some legends, the little baby began to walk as soon as he was born! He took seven steps, and with each step, a lotus flower blossomed in the ground. After he took his seventh step, he suddenly uttered, 'This is my last birth. There will be no more births for me.'

Of course, this is hard to believe, for how can a newborn baby walk, or even speak? But the life of the Buddha is full of such legends.

The Supreme Sakyan

Back at the palace, King Shudhodhana paced up and down anxiously, waiting for news. Finally an out-of-breath messenger arrived.

'It's a boy!' he announced, his face wreathed in smiles. 'Queen Mahamaya has given birth to a baby boy.'

King Shudhodhana was so thrilled that he yanked a pearl necklace off his neck and gifted it to the messenger. He could barely wait for the queen to come back.

As soon as the queen returned, there was joyous celebration in the kingdom.

'He is beautiful,' the king said rapturously when he saw his infant son for the first time. 'We shall name him Siddhartha. He will be a fine king and make the kingdom of Sakya famous the world over.' The queen smiled happily.

The happy parents had no idea how true the king's words were going to be, though not in the sense he had meant them. The young prince Siddhartha did indeed grow up to become renowned all over the world. Only not as a king, but as an inspiring teacher and the founder of one of the world's greatest religions—Buddhism.

A Dream That Would Come True

One night, much before Siddhartha had been born, Queen Mahamaya had had a dream. In her dream, an elephant came down from the heavens. He told her that she was about to become pregnant and that she would have a baby boy who would become a great man. Sure enough, she was soon with child and little Siddhartha was born.

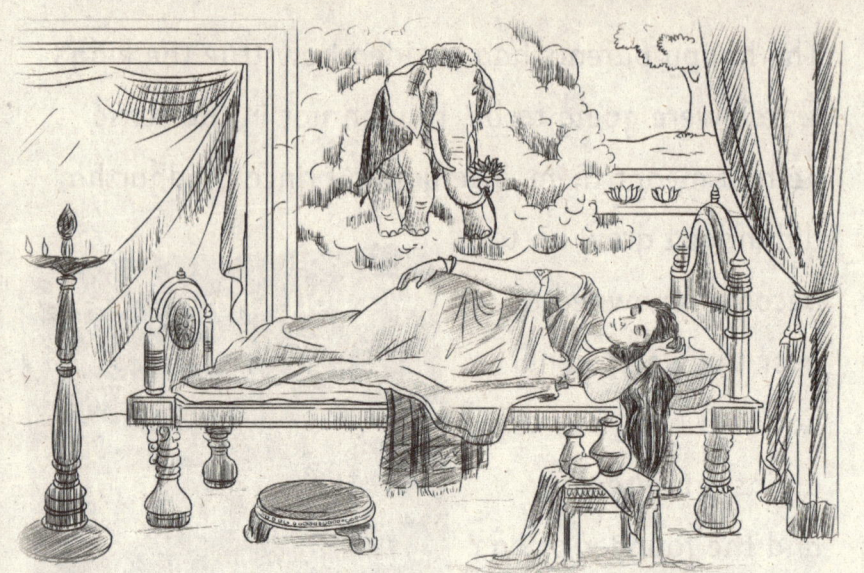

King Shudhodhana had been excited to hear of
the queen's dream. When the baby was born,
he decided to find out what the vision meant.

'I will take our son to my old guru, Asita.
He is very wise and knows about such things,'
he decided.

Meanwhile, deep in the jungles, Asita the sage,
while meditating one evening, is said to have
suddenly seen the devas dancing joyously.

'Why are you so happy?' he asked the gods.

'We are happy because an extraordinary being has been born to Queen Mahamaya in Lumbini.
He will change the life of millions,' they sang.

When Asita heard this, he went to Kapilavastu at once to see his old student Shudhodhana.

When the king saw Asita, he was astounded.
'How did you know I wanted you to see my son, Gurudev?' he asked.

Asita merely smiled. He held out his hands for the little prince. But the baby turned away, his feet pointing towards the sage.

When Asita saw the prince's feet, he fell silent. For on them he saw a pattern that told him something.

'This is no ordinary prince. He will become a great teacher one day—the greatest in the world,' Asita announced.

> **Oh Really?**
> The king went on to touch his son's feet many more times in his life after he realized what a wise and noble man he was.

King Shudhodhana was delighted. He touched his son's feet. It was the first time the king touched the feet of the great Buddha.

Blessing the Baby

It was time to bless the newborn. A grand feast was planned and, as was the custom, five wise men were invited to bless the child.

After the ceremony was completed, the wise men examined the birthmarks on the child. They studied the baby for a while and finally gave their verdict.

'This child will be the king of all kings . . . if he so chooses,' one of the learned men announced.

'But if he chooses not to, he will become the wisest in the world. A Buddha,' a second scholar added.

The king was taken aback. He was sure he wanted Siddhartha to be a king. He didn't like the idea of him becoming a Buddha. The king was about to say something when the youngest of the five men spoke up.

'He will *never* be a king. He will definitely be a Buddha. That is a certainty!' he concluded.

Did You Know?
A Buddha is a person who has attained the ultimate wisdom or knowledge and has no worldly attachments. It is a state of complete perfection in every sense of the word. There are many Buddhas, but there is only one Gautama Buddha. Gautama is the name that identifies him as coming from the Sakyan tribe and thus different from the other Buddhas. Some also called him Sakyamuni, which means hermit of the Sakya tribe.

'If the prince ever sees a sick person, an aged person, a dead body or a monk, he will give up his princehood at once and instead want to become a monk himself,' he went on to warn the king.

Now the king was worried. He didn't want his son to be a sage or an ascetic. He wanted him to become the greatest king the world had ever seen. And so he resolved to shield Siddhartha from all things unpleasant.

2 A Life of Luxury

Siddhartha grew up in the lap of incredible luxury. He had just about everything he needed. Sadly, though, his mother, Queen Mahamaya, died when he was just a few days old. He was brought up by his aunt, Prajapati Gautami.

Oh Really?

Prajapati Gautami, who was Queen Mahamaya's sister, gave birth to a son on the very day Queen Mahamaya died. But she loved Siddhartha so much that she gave him more attention than she did to her own son, Nanda.

Boyhood Years

Soon it was time to send Siddhartha to school. King Shudhodhana made sure the prince went to an exclusive school, along with the children of other noblemen. The students were taught languages, maths, science and geography. They also learnt skills like boxing, archery and wrestling. Young Siddhartha seemed to master everything with the greatest ease.

It's True!

When Siddhartha was quite young, he attended a ploughing ceremony. During the affair, suddenly no one could find him. Everyone searched everywhere and finally, the boy was spotted sitting in silent thought under a tree. He must have been just seven or eight years old at the time.

'He is remarkable,' his teacher Sarva Mitra reported to the king. 'He is smart, eager and respectful. He is the fastest learner in the entire school.'

The king was pleased. Siddhartha was turning out just as he hoped.

One day, an incident occurred that should have given the king and Siddhartha's teachers a peek at how life was going to turn out for the prince.

The boys were practising archery in the protected woods (for Siddhartha was never allowed to step outside the palace gates lest he saw any of the sights his father had been warned against). His cousin Devadatta, who was with him, spotted a swan flying across the sky. Without telling his cousin what he was about to do, Devadatta took aim and shot at the bird. His aim was perfect and the swan was hit.

As the injured bird came tumbling down, a distraught Siddhartha rushed towards it.

He cradled it in his arms, wanting desperately to heal it.

'How could you do such a cruel thing?' he cried out to Devadatta.

'Leave the swan. *I've* shot it down, so it's *my* bird to do with as I wish,' retorted Devadatta.

But Siddhartha would not let it go. He gently pulled the arrow out and tried to stop the bleeding. Just then, their guru Sarva Mitra came along to see what the matter was.

The boys brought the issue before Sarva Mitra. The guru listened carefully and then smiled.

'Life itself is meant to be saved. And so it will belong to the one who tries to save it, not to the one who destroys it,' he replied. 'Siddhartha, the bird is yours.'

This was only a small episode, yet it showed the love and compassion Siddhartha had for all living things.

Despite the prince's kind nature, King
Shudhodhana was worried. All the while,
the words of the wise men haunted him.

'I must take care that Siddhartha never sees a sick
person, an old person, a dead body or a monk,'
he reminded himself every day. He employed
servants, singers and
musicians to take
care of Siddhartha's
every need. And he
never allowed any
sick or aged people
or monks in
his palace.

Oh Really?

King Shudhodhana was so careful
that he built three palaces for
young Siddhartha—a winter
palace, a summer palace and
even one for the rains. He also
acquired hunting grounds and
parks so that the prince would
never feel the need to step outside
the palace grounds.

A Restless Mind

And so it was that Siddhartha had everything a young man could want. He had friends, luxury and entertainment. He had the best teachers and plenty of books to read. But strangely, he felt discontented. He'd always been a thoughtful young boy. But now it seemed as if thinking was all he did.

'There must be more to life than all this singing and dancing and having a good time,' he would wonder. He would spend hours looking out of the window. He would listlessly wander about the vast gardens of the palace. He felt very uneasy, as if something were missing.

'Oh, what am I to do with this boy?' King Shudhodhana thought despairingly to himself. He decided to seek the counsel of his ministers.

'Prince Siddhartha is unhappy,' he explained to them. 'What do you think I should do to cheer him up?'

'Get him married,' came the reply. 'A nice young bride will definitely cheer him up and steer his thoughts in a happier direction!'

The ministers were convinced that this was the solution to the problem. The boy was sixteen years old, and surely a pretty young girl for a wife would distract him.

The king thought it was an excellent idea. He made an announcement calling for all the beautiful and accomplished girls in the kingdom.

Naturally, there was great excitement, for Siddhartha was known for his handsome looks and good nature.

> ## Oh Really?
>
> It is said that when Siddhartha was in his teens, he was sent to study at Takshashila University. This was one of the world's first great universities, where students were taught advanced subjects like astronomy, medicine, mathematics and other sciences. The ruins of this ancient university are near present-day Rawalpindi in Pakistan.

A Match Written in the Stars

In the neighbouring kingdom, a young girl of the same age heard this news. Her name was Yashodhara. She had heard much about Siddhartha all her life, even though she had never actually met him. From her brother, Yashodhara had heard the story of the injured swan and Siddhartha's soft heart.

'I would like to marry such a man,' she thought. She decided to meet Siddhartha. When she told her father about her wishes, he grew worried.

'Oh, daughter,'
he said, 'you must
have heard what
they say about
Siddhartha. It is said
he is a Buddha and
that one day he will
leave everything
behind to become a monk. What will you
do then?'

'Father,' replied Yashodhara, 'I do know of this.
But I will marry no other. I feel I know Siddhartha
from a previous life. It is our destiny to
be married.'

Her father had no choice. And sure enough,
when Siddhartha laid his eyes on Yashodhara
among the scores of other damsels, he walked
towards her without hesitation. He gave her
an ornament to indicate that he had chosen her
as his bride.

It was an extravagant
wedding with the
celebrations lasting
many days. Even
though Yashodhara
knew in her heart that

It's True!
Yashodhara was known by
many names. Among them
were Gopa, Subhaddaka,
Bhaddaka and Bimba.

one day her husband would leave her and all his
worldly belongings, she resolved to make the most
of their short life together.

21

3 The Four Sights

Siddhartha and Yashodhara led a happy married life for thirteen years. They felt that they had known each other in their past lives too—that's how close they were. They did all the things that young couples do. They laughed, discussed ideas and read books together. Yashodhara understood Siddhartha's confusion and even shared some of his feelings. But even through all the experiences of marital life, that old sense of unease Siddhartha felt never left him.

One day, destiny took a turn, as it was meant to. Tired of being enclosed behind the gigantic walls that surrounded the palace property, Siddhartha asked for his father's permission to step into the city.

'Father, as a prince I must know more about our people. I wish to walk around the city,' he said to the king.

Knowing that there was no reason by which he could hold Siddhartha back, the king was forced to agree. 'Give me a few days, and then you may visit the city,' he told his son.

But King Shudhodhana did not stray from his resolve. He was buying some time so he could rid the city of all unpleasantness. He ordered every street to be decorated, and for old and sick people to be kept at home, all so that Siddhartha would not lay his eyes on them.

An Old Man

Finally, Siddhartha drove out of the gates along with Channa, his charioteer. Everywhere he went, he saw people dressed well and looking happy. The town looked cheerful and celebratory.

But suddenly he saw a sight he had never seen before. A beggar had wandered into the city from another village. He was very old and very thin— so thin that his bones stuck out all along his frail

body. His eyes were sunken and he was weak from
staggering around. In his hand was an empty bowl
and he was begging for some food.

Siddhartha simply stared. He had never
encountered such a man in his entire life.

'Who is that, Channa? And why does he tremble
so?' he asked.

'Your Majesty, that is an old man. He seems to
be a beggar,' Channa replied.

'What's an old man . . . and what's a beggar?'
Siddhartha demanded. The charioteer knew at
once that the prince had seen something he should
not have.

'Your Majesty, i-it's n-nothing! It is just that,
um . . . we grow old and sometimes become weak.
And . . . some people are rich and have everything
they need. But some are so poor that they have to
beg for food from those who have it. Now let us go
back!' Channa quickly turned the chariot around
and drove home to the safety of the palace.

But the damage had been done. Siddhartha
couldn't get the picture of the old beggar out of
his mind. He resolved to go out into the city once
again, but without telling his father.

A Sick Man

Having dressed up as a common man, he
persuaded Channa to drive him to the city. This
time, the city had not been prepared, for no one
knew the prince was coming.

Siddhartha watched, enchanted, as ordinary people went about their business, when he heard a shout.

'Go away!' A man was shouting at someone lying on the ground.

Siddhartha went closer to see what was happening. To his horror, he saw a man in torn clothes writhing on the street, near a gutter. Other people were trying to stay away from him. What was worse was that the man was covered in sores and boils from which pus and blood were oozing out.

'Stay away from him, Your Majesty,' Channa begged Siddhartha, trying to pull him away from the dreadful sight. 'You might catch his disease!'

'This man is in pain,' protested Siddhartha. 'I must help him.'

But Channa dragged him away. Siddhartha grew distraught.

'Why are we going away? And what was the matter with that man?' he asked.

Channa realized there was no way he could avoid answering his prince. 'Your Majesty, he has an illness called leprosy. It is a very painful disease,' he explained.

'And are there many such diseases?' demanded Siddhartha.

'Hundreds of diseases,' replied Channa. 'And we will all get some illness or the other at some point in our lives.'

Now Siddhartha was cast into even greater confusion. Why were some people ill and some not? Why were some rich and some poor? Back at the palace, he became silent and withdrawn.

A Dead Body

He told his father that he was going to visit the city right away. The king realized he could not stop Siddhartha. Once more the prince set forth with Channa, this time dressed as a nobleman.

As they roamed the streets, looking at the people, a procession came into view. A moving group of people were carrying a sleeping man on their shoulders. They were chanting something and many of them were weeping.

'What is happening?' Siddhartha asked Channa. 'Why is that man sleeping on their shoulders? And why are they carrying him?'

'Your Majesty, that is a funeral procession. That man isn't sleeping. He is . . . dead,' Channa replied cautiously.

'*Dead?* Are we all going to be dead some day?'
Siddhartha asked, mystified. He was troubled
but also intrigued.

'Yes, Your Majesty. All living things must die some
day,' Channa explained.

A thousand questions arose in Siddhartha's mind.
Why do we die? Where do we go when we die?
Are we born again?

A Monk

When he got home, he went straight to his room and stayed cooped up for an entire week. He spoke to no one of what he'd seen, not even to Yashodhara, with whom he could usually talk freely about anything. All Siddhartha wanted to do was think. When he finally emerged, he was determined to go into the city and see more of what life was really all about. The king watched in despair. He knew now that the prophecy of Siddhartha becoming a Buddha was coming true.

Siddhartha and Channa walked miles and miles through the city streets. The prince discovered life for what it was. There were happy people, but there were also people who looked sad. There were healthy people, but there were also people with dreadful diseases.

As he walked, he came across a man dressed in strange orange robes. He had nothing in his hand,

except a stick and a bowl. His face was perfectly calm and a smile played on his lips.

'Who is that man?' demanded Siddhartha. 'Of all the people I have seen, he looks the most tranquil.'

'That is a monk, O Prince,' Channa replied. 'He has given up all his worldly belongings. He eats what people give him but he wants nothing.'

Siddhartha was struck by how peaceful the man looked. 'I wish I could be like that man,' he thought to himself.

Siddhartha walked many miles and finally stopped to rest under a tree. But his mind would simply not rest. There were too many questions popping up, to which he needed answers.

His next step was clear. He needed his questions answered by someone who had the right knowledge.

4 Giving Up the Royal Life

When Siddhartha reached home after his adventures in the city, he found the entire palace in a state of high excitement.

'What is happening?' he asked his attendants.

'Your Majesty, Princess Yashodhara has given birth to a baby boy,' they gushed.

Just then King Shudhodhana appeared, his face radiant. 'Congratulations, my son! You are now the father of a beautiful boy,' he exclaimed, embracing Siddhartha.

> **It's True!**
> Siddhartha and his wife were both twenty-nine years old when their son was born.

Siddhartha blinked. This *was* wonderful news, but why did he not feel elated, as he should've been? He went to see his newborn son. The entire kingdom was celebrating the birth of a new prince, but Siddhartha was still troubled. What was the matter with him?

That night, there was a grand feast. The king had organized entertainment and the finest food and drink for all the guests. Everyone in court was singing, dancing, eating and drinking. But when Siddhartha saw the merriment around him, all he could think of were the four sights he had seen.

'How can the material things in life bring us eternal joy?' Siddhartha wondered. 'Surely these things will end some day? And then what?'

Oh Really?
Siddhartha named his son Rahula. In Pali—an early language—Rahula means bond. It is said that Siddhartha felt Rahula might be the bond that would prevent him from giving up worldly pleasures.

A Prince Becomes a Pauper

Siddhartha was restless throughout the celebrations. He fell asleep early and was haunted by troubling dreams. Late that night, he awoke bathed in sweat.

'I cannot handle this unrest any more!' he thought. 'I must go out and find the answers to all my questions.' He decided to leave the palace at once.

He tiptoed into Yashodhara's chambers. His wife was sleeping peacefully with her infant son next to her. Siddhartha looked down at the sleeping figures. He didn't dare touch them for fear of waking them up. He didn't want to be deterred from going on his quest.

Silently, he left the palace with the trusted Channa. He rode his favourite horse, Kanthaka, for the last time.

When they'd reached the heart of the forest, Siddhartha halted. He removed all his jewellery and fine clothes. Instead, he wore a simple orange robe, wrapped loosely around himself.

'Take these and go back to the palace,' he told Channa.

Channa was beside himself with grief.

'O my lord, please take me with you!' he begged. But Siddhartha would have none of it.

Oh Really?
It is believed that the faithful Channa never got over his sorrow at his separation from Siddhartha. Some say he died a few years later and never saw his beloved prince as the Buddha, while others say he became a monk himself and followed the Buddha's teachings for the rest of his life.

He walked further into the forest, not looking back even once. For Siddhartha, that was the end of one life but the beginning of another. He was on his way to becoming a Buddha.

An Offer and a Promise

Siddhartha walked miles and miles, from village to village and city to city. He ate the alms people gave him. One day, he found himself in Rajagraha (now known as Rajgir, in present-day Bihar), the capital of the kingdom of Magadha, of which King Bimbisara was the ruler. By now, people had heard of the Sakyan prince who had become an ascetic.

Siddhartha was sitting under a tree in deep reflection when a messenger went running to King Bimbisara's court.

'Your Majesty, the strange Sakyan mendicant, who was once a prince, has come to Magadha!' he reported breathlessly.

King Bimbisara stood up. He knew Siddhartha's family and wanted to meet him. He went to Siddhartha and asked him, 'Why are you doing this? It must grieve your father greatly. Come and live here in Magadha, and I will give you half my kingdom.'

But Siddhartha merely smiled. 'My mission is to find the answer to how we can be free of death and illness,' he replied. 'I must not stop.'

'In that case, promise me that you will return to Rajagraha some day after you have found your answers,' the king requested.

After promising the king that he would return, Siddhartha was on his way again.

The Quest for a Teacher

Siddhartha was becoming better known as Gautama, which was a family name. Later, this would help differentiate him from the other Buddhas. Now Gautama was looking for a guru who would help him on his path. And he did meet some great spiritual teachers.

From one called Alara Kalama he learnt how to meditate. Soon he knew more than his teacher. So he went on his way to learn further.

Did You Know?
Meditation requires sitting still in total silence for long periods of time. During meditation, the mind is not supposed to think of worldly things like food or work. Instead, the mind goes into deeper thoughts that help understand oneself and the world.

He discovered another great teacher, called
Uddaka, who was well known for his wisdom.
Once more, Gautama learnt well and quickly. But
Uddaka could not answer Gautama's questions on
how one could stop suffering, old age or death.
Thus it was time to move on once again and find
someone who could teach him more.

The Five Friends

Gautama had learnt a lot but he still had no answers to his original questions—how to be free from death, illness and sorrow. So he walked on. Along his journey he met five men, who, like him, had given up a life of luxury in the quest to find answers to life's questions.

They were Bhaddiya, Vappa, Kondanna, Mahanama and Assaji. They too were ascetics, who had chosen to seek the truth by torturing their bodies. They felt that by hurting their bodies, their minds would be free. Craving for answers, Gautama too tried this extreme technique.

He decided to fast. He would subsist on a single grain of rice a day. He became as thin as a stick and had no energy. But no flash of light or understanding appeared, and he was no wiser than before. Gautama tried another technique of depriving his body, by holding his breath. He went without air till his ears and nose bled. But through all this, he found no answers.

For six long years Gautama tried all kinds of methods to torture his body without succumbing to pain. But finally, he decided all these experiments were doing him no good. He was no closer to the answers to his questions than he was when he'd left home. He decided to put a stop to this. His five ascetic friends were disappointed in him, thinking that he had given up his quest.

But far from giving up, Gautama was off to try newer methods.

5 Seeing the Light

After wandering around for days and nights, Gautama found himself near a large peepul tree. Something about the tree called out to him. He made a resolution.

'I shall sit under this tree and meditate upon my questions. And I shall not move until I have my answers. Even if my skin rots and my body decays, I shall not budge till I see the light,' he decided.

He sat in the lotus position, closed his eyes and concentrated on his breathing. As the night passed, he went through many different feelings.

The Temptation of Mara

First, the evil demon Mara came to him. Mara tried his best to tempt Gautama away from his pursuit. He painted pictures of wealth and beauty. He tried to scare him with awful images of starvation and death. But Gautama remained steadfast, not tempted nor scared. Finally, Mara gave up and went away.

Gautama sat deep in profound meditation. He felt as if he was floating. Suddenly, he could see the world as if from far, far

away. He saw himself. He saw that he had died many times before and that he had been reborn each time. He saw all his past lives. He saw all the things he had done in his lives—the good as well as the bad. And finally, he realized something.

The Enlightenment

Gautama realized that people are born again when they desire things. Specifically, the bad things they do in their former lives cause them to come back to earth in a new life, as if to correct them. But the people who realize this and free themselves of desire—those who want nothing from life—are finally free from the cycle of birth and death. That's when they reach nirvana, the perfect heaven.

Of course, all this was in Gautama's mind while his body sat still, which seemed to glow brilliantly from within. At that moment, Gautama had become a Buddha. He had seen the light.

WHAT IS NIRVANA?

Nirvana, according to Buddhism, is the state in which the mind is at complete peace and the soul is merged with the universe. It is reached when a person's desires and suffering all go away and they need nor want nothing.

The Next Seven Weeks

For the next seven weeks, the Buddha continued to sit in silence, allowing his mind and spirit to understand what he had just seen.

During the first week, the Buddha was happy and content, feeling true peace for the first time.

Oh Really?
Even now, it is customary for Buddhists to pay homage to the Bodhi tree that canopied the Buddha, as well as the offshoots of the tree.

During the second week, he felt a deep gratitude to the peepul tree that had sheltered him as he'd sought the light.

During the third week, the Buddha saw the devas. Not sure if they were indeed gods, he built a golden bridge in the air and walked across it to the heavens.

During the fourth week, he created a special chamber in which he meditated. His mind and body became so pure that it is said to have radiated bright rays in six different colours—blue, orange, red, white, yellow and a combination of these five colours. These colours stood for purity, confidence, wisdom, the lack of desire and

Did You Know?
The Buddhist flag is in these six colours.

holiness. The five colours together stood for all these qualities.

During the fifth week, three beautiful girls appeared, who tried their best to distract the Buddha and lure him away from his thoughts. Their names were Raga, Rati and Tanha. But no matter how much they tried, the Buddha remained unmoved.

During the sixth week, the Buddha went to meditate at the foot of the Mucalinda tree. It began to rain and the air was freezing. That's when an enormous king cobra called Mucalinda appeared and coiled himself around the Buddha seven times. Then he raised his hood and covered the Buddha, keeping him warm and dry.

During the seventh week, two merchants called Tapussa and Bhallika appeared. The Buddha, seated under the Rajayatana tree, had been fasting for

Oh Really?
The strand of hair that the Buddha is said to have given Tapussa and Bhallika is enshrined in a Buddhist pagoda in Yangon, Myanmar.

forty-nine days by then. They brought rice cakes and honey to help him break his fast. When the Buddha explained what he had experienced, they were entranced. They became his first ordinary followers, and the Buddha gave them a strand of hair from his head as a token.

6 Teaching the World

The Buddha wanted to share his knowledge with others. He wanted the whole world to be free from desire and the fear of death. He remembered his five friends who were also on a quest. He heard that they were living in the city of Benares (now called Varanasi) and so he set off to search for them.

He found them living in a grove in a deer park, at a site called Sarnath. Kondanna, Bhaddiya, Vappa, Mahanama and Assaji saw him approaching.

'Hah, he's back!' they snorted derisively. They hadn't forgiven him for abandoning their methods of torturing the body to attain realization.

But as the Buddha came closer, they were struck by the difference in him. Gone was the doubtful, confused man. There seemed to be a radiance and glow about this man. And his face reflected a kind of peace they had never seen on anyone.

'My friends,' the Buddha said, 'I have come to share with you what I have learnt.' And he began to speak. He told them his realizations in what became his first-ever discourse or lecture.

'You must follow the middle path,' he explained. 'Neither torturing oneself nor indulgence is the right way.' Then he elaborated on the Four Noble Truths and the Eightfold Path, which would lead them to the light too.

THE FOUR NOBLE TRUTHS

1. There is suffering in the world.

2. The cause of suffering is craving and desire.

3. Suffering and the cycle of rebirth ends when you attain nirvana.

4. The way to achieve nirvana is to follow the Eightfold Path.

THE NOBLE EIGHTFOLD PATH

1. The right understanding (which is to know the Four Truths)

2. The right attitude (which is being able to let go of desires, to think well of others, to be harmless and never cruel)

3. The right speech (which is to never tell untruths, or gossip or be nasty)

4. The right action (which is to never kill, steal from or harm anyone)

5. The right livelihood (which is to avoid businesses that can harm anyone or anything)

6. The right effort (which is by not thinking evil thoughts and thinking only positive thoughts)

7. The right mindfulness (which is being aware of one's feelings and duties)

8. The right concentration (which is by being focused)

The knowledge and practice of this path is called dhamma (or dharma).

More and More Followers

Everywhere the Buddha went with his message, he gathered followers—monks and disciples called bhikkhus. He remembered his promise to King Bimbisara and went to Rajagraha. There he spent some months preaching to the people of Magadha. When King Bimbisara heard him, he too became an avid follower and, right till his death, remained a staunch supporter. King Bimbisara even provided land on which the Buddha's followers built a rest house.

The Buddha's fame eventually reached the ears of King Shudhodhana. He knew at once that this was none other than Siddhartha, his own son. He decided to meet the Buddha. When the king reached the place where the Buddha was preaching, he was astounded to see large crowds listening to the monk's sermon.

But the king grew disturbed when he saw the Buddha receiving alms from people.

'Oh, Siddhartha, why do you accept food from people?' he lamented. 'You are shaming me.'

'Father, there is no shame in what I am doing,' the Buddha replied. He explained that the alms that his disciples gave the monks were a mark of respect and not of charity. He also explained the dhamma he had discovered. When the king finally understood what the Buddha was teaching, he too was converted.

The sangha, or the group of the Buddha's followers, kept growing. Over the course of time, his stepmother, his cousins and his old friends—all joined his school of thought and became monks.

Rahula's Inheritance

When the Buddha was in Kapilavastu, Yashodhara, his wife, heard the news and sent for their son, Rahula, to meet him.

'Go to your father and ask him for your inheritance,' she told him.

When Rahula went to the Buddha and asked him for his inheritance, the Buddha thought for a while.

'By giving him my worldly inheritance, I will simply be giving him sorrow and troubles. It's better that I give him the inheritance of my learning,' he decided.

So he made Rahula a monk, who was not even ten years of age at the time. This upset the Buddha's

father, King Shudhodhana. The king made the Buddha promise that he would never take anyone into the order of monks without taking the permission of their parents.

Did You Know?

When Yashodhara heard of the life Siddhartha had embraced, she too gave up all her worldly belongings. Though she continued to live in the palace, she gave up her fine clothes and jewellery and wore a simple sari instead; she would eat just one meal a day and spend a lot of time in meditation. Finally, she too joined the Buddha's order, becoming a nun, or a bhikkhuni.

THE BUDDHA'S ROUTINE

The Buddha followed a very strict schedule. His day was divided into five parts:

- The morning session: He would rise at 4 a.m. and meditate. Then he would observe the world with his mind's eye and see who needed help. He would then step out and ask for alms.

- The afternoon session: From 12 noon to 6 p.m., he would listen to the questions and problems of monks as well as ordinary people. He would teach them the principles of dhamma.

- The first watch: From 6 p.m. to 10 p.m., he would meet his followers once again and spend time with them.

- The middle watch: From 10 p.m. to 2 a.m. in the night, the devas would come to meet the Buddha.

- The last watch: From 2 a.m. to 4 a.m., the Buddha would meditate and free himself from the troubles of the day. He would also sleep for an hour sometime in between, before he awoke again.

Against the Buddha

Even though the Buddha had numerous followers, there were plenty who were against him. They did not like the power that he wielded over so many people.

That's Amazing!
The Buddha wandered through the country, spreading dhamma, for over forty-five years. Through all that time, he would sleep for just one hour every night.

One day, such a group of people decided to do something about it. They called upon a female ascetic called Sundari and convinced her to visit the Buddha every day. When they saw that people had noticed that she was a follower of the Buddha, they quietly killed her and buried her body. When some disciples of the Buddha discovered her body, they thought the Buddha or his followers had done it.

'This man is a fake!' some said.

'These monks are murderers!' added others.

But the majority of the people simply refused to believe that either the Buddha or any of his followers could do anything so terrible. And instead of his followers dwindling, their numbers simply grew and grew. For the next few decades, the Buddha moved from place to place, preaching, healing and spreading his message.

7 Achieving Nirvana

The Buddha was now almost eighty years old. He had been preaching for more than forty-five of them. His mind was as young as ever, but his body had become old. He decided he had accomplished what he had set out to do and that it was time for him to leave the earth.

The Buddha decided to spend the last year of his life in the peaceful surroundings of a small village called Kusinara (now called Kushinagar, in present-day Uttar Pradesh). He didn't want to live in large cities any more. Many of his closest friends and even his wife, Yashodhara, and son, Rahula, had passed away. He was only worried about one thing now—how would the monks carry on after he was no more?

Finally, one day, he decided it was time. Ananda, his most faithful follower, was with him.

'Ananda,' the Buddha told him, 'make me a bed between two sal trees. I want to lie down.'

Ananda immediately realized what the Buddha was saying. He knew it was time for him to go. Ananda broke down and began crying inconsolably.

'Ananda,' chided the Buddha, 'you cannot cry. Haven't I taught you? There is no separation from those we love. Now go into Kusinara and spread the word of my departure.'

All of the Buddha's most trusted followers gathered around him as he spoke to them for the last time.

'My brothers,' said the Buddha, 'remember this. All material things in this world change. Nothing lasts. You must work hard for your own peace and salvation.' Saying this, he closed his eyes and went into deep meditation, free of all desires and ties. His soul rose, leaving his body. And the Buddha left this earth for the last time.

And so, on a full moon night in May, Gautama Buddha achieved nirvana.

8 Life after the Buddha

After the Buddha passed on, his followers were plunged into grief. But there was one monk who refused to mourn—he rejoiced instead.

'Brothers,' he tried to explain to the others, 'we must not grieve. Our beloved Buddha has achieved salvation. It is now up to us to spread his teachings far and wide.'

The First Buddhist Council

All the monks decided to have a great meeting to decide how to move forward. King Ajatashatru of Magadha, who supported the Buddha with all his heart, made arrangements for an assembly of the sangha at the Sattapani Cave in Rajagraha. Five hundred seats were laid out and five hundred enlightened bhikkhus (called arhats) came for the meeting. This was the first Buddhist council, during which the rules for the male and female monks were decided.

Did You Know?
Ananda, one of the Buddha's most faithful followers, had not yet become an arhat at the time of the Buddha's death. The night before the council, he meditated with all his heart and soul. By morning, he had achieved enlightenment and was able to attend the meeting as an arhat.

The tenets arrived at during the council came to be known as the Pali Tripitaka. In those faraway days, scriptures were not written down but passed on orally. Many centuries later, a great Buddhist king from Sri Lanka, called Vatta Gamani Abhaya, called another council. The Tripitaka was then written down in Pali on ola palm leaves. Through the centuries, they were handed down by the monks to their next generation.

Emperor Ashoka Propagates Buddhism

Though the Buddha was no longer on this earth, his followers kept increasing in number. Great kings like Emperor Ashoka, ruler of the vast Mauryan Empire, converted to Buddhism. Ashoka carved many Buddhist edicts on stupas (dome-shaped shrines) and built viharas (monasteries) all over India and

Oh Really?

Emperor Ashoka was a fierce and powerful king. One day, he witnessed a horrific battle in which thousands of soldiers were killed. He was so disturbed by the sight of the dead and injured that he became a Buddhist, following a religion that totally shunned violence of any kind.

the neighbouring countries. He also developed universities where Buddhism was taught.

Buddhism in the Far East

Trade relations between India and the Han dynasty of China strengthened during the first century BCE. The Chinese experienced the power of Buddhism and many converted. Some Chinese scholars, such as Dao'an, translated Buddhist texts into Chinese. Buddhist art, architecture and literature flourished in China as king after king supported Buddhism. Today, China has the largest Buddhist population in the world.

Not content with just spreading Buddhism in China, several Chinese monks went to neighbouring countries to spread the Buddha's teachings. Many Korean monks were so inspired that they went to China to learn more. Soon Korea too had a large Buddhist following.

The king of Paekche, a Korean kingdom, wishing to improve relations with Japan, sent a gift of the Buddha's image along with copies of Buddhist texts to the Japanese emperor. The Japanese were so struck by the beliefs of Buddhism that they adopted it along with their own Shinto beliefs. Many Japanese royals supported Buddhism wholeheartedly and numerous Buddhist temples

were built. Prince Shotoku was one such royal who did a lot to spread Buddhism in Japan.

Soon Buddhism spread across all of Asia. Every country that had a large Buddhist following sent missionaries into other countries to spread the word of the Buddha. In Western countries, however, Buddhism—though practised by some—has not become as widespread as in Asia.

Buddhism Today

Today, Buddhism is an important religion in so many countries: China, Japan, Thailand, Vietnam, Myanmar, Sri Lanka, South Korea, Taiwan, Cambodia and, of course, India are all countries with countless Buddhist followers.

The quest of a prince to find the answers to his questions led to the birth of one of humanity's greatest religions—one that has millions of followers all over the world.

Did You Know?

Buddhism has four main pilgrimage sites:

1. Lumbini, Nepal: This is Gautama Buddha's birthplace.

2. Bodhgaya, India: This spot is believed to be where the Buddha attained enlightenment under the Bodhi tree. The Mahabodhi Temple, which is the most important Buddhist religious centre, is located here.

3. Sarnath, India: This is where the Buddha delivered his first sermon.

4. Kushinagar, India: This is where the Buddha breathed his last.

9 Tales That Touch

Gautama Buddha touched millions of lives through his teachings—people he never met and many who were born thousands of years after he passed on. But during his lifetime too, there were many whose lives he changed in incredible ways. Let's meet some of them and read their stories.

Angulimala, the Bandit

There was once a man called Bhaggawa, who lived in the kingdom of Kosala. On the day his wife gave birth to a baby boy, miraculously, all the weapons in the land began to shine. Everyone was puzzled. Bhaggawa decided to call his son Ahimsaka (the non-violent one) because his birth was connected with weapons.

When Ahimsaka grew up, he went to the University of Takshashila. He was such a good student that he beat all the other students in every subject. But instead of being proud of his student, his teacher was threatened by him. As *gurudakshina* (a gift demanded by the guru, which cannot be refused), the teacher asked Ahimsaka for a necklace made of a thousand human fingers, each from a different victim.

Ahimsaka was in a quandary. But he had to fulfil his guru's wish. So he began to hide in forests and attack passers-by. He would kill them and cut off a finger to add to his collection. Thus he collected 999 fingers and needed just one more. Ahimsaka soon became known as Angulimala (meaning a necklace made of fingers).

People were terrified. The king ordered Angulimala to be killed. When his mother, Mantani, heard of this, she knew it was her son. She decided to confront him and walked into the forest. When Angulimala saw his mother, he didn't know what to do. His promise to his guru was driving his actions. He was about to kill her, when the Buddha appeared.

Angulimala reached for his sword to kill the Buddha instead, but the Buddha kept out of his reach even though he wasn't moving at all! Angulimala was stunned. That's when the Buddha stopped the bandit. He told Angulimala about the Four Truths and the Eightfold Path.

Angulimala fell at the Buddha's feet. He finally saw the error of his ways. He became a monk and followed the Buddha till the end of his days.

The Serpent King

In his early days, when he had just sixty disciples, Gautama Buddha was on his way to the kingdom of Magadha. During the journey, he passed by a settlement on the banks of a river, where three brothers lived with their followers. Their names were Uruvela Kassapa, Nadi Kassapa and Gaya Kassapa.

Wanting his monks to rest a bit, the Buddha requested Uruvela Kassapa for permission to stay in his hut.

'I can sleep in your kitchen,' said the Buddha.

'I would be happy if you stayed with me,' replied Uruvela. 'But there is a fierce and nasty serpent king who lives in the nether regions of my kitchen. He will harm you.'

The Buddha merely smiled. 'If you do not object, I will be happy to stay,' he said.

As night fell and the Buddha settled down in

the kitchen, the serpent king slithered out to see what was happening. He hissed and snarled at the Buddha. But the Buddha, instead of retaliating, simply smiled. He sent the serpent rays of love. The angrier the serpent became, the more the Buddha showed his love. Finally, the serpent gave up. He was moved by the Buddha, and he coiled up peacefully for the night.

The next morning, Uruvela Kassapa was astonished to see the Buddha safe and sound and the fierce serpent lying next to him as gentle as a lamb.

'How did you do it?' Uruvela Kassapa demanded.

'Would you like to know the secret of calming the most violent creatures?' the Buddha asked.

Then he told Uruvela Kassapa the secret of dhamma. And from that day on, Uruvela Kassapa and his brothers became ardent followers of the Buddha.

Alavaka, the Demon

There was once a ferocious demon living in the hills near the kingdom of Kosala. He was known to be a cannibal, one who eats human flesh. He terrorized all the people around. One day, he captured the king of Alavi. The king begged to be released, and the demon agreed to do so only on the condition that the king would send him one human every day as food.

The king agreed. He ordered his prisoners to be sent first, one day at a time, to the demon. Soon the jails were empty. The king then started sending the men of the village. Soon there were no men left. He went on like this until there was no one left, except his own son.

With a heavy heart, the king decided to sacrifice his son too. When the Buddha heard of this, he immediately went to Alavaka's abode in the mountains. Alavaka was not home, so the Buddha entered and began preaching to the demon's many wives.

Alavaka soon returned. When he saw the Buddha, he was furious.

'Who are you and what are you doing here?' he thundered. 'Do you want to be eaten like the rest?'

'I am explaining something important to your wives,' the Buddha replied calmly.

'Oho! You are a wise man, are you? Well, then, answer my questions and I might let you go,' Alavaka roared.

This is how their conversation went:

'What is the greatest wealth?'

'Confidence is the most valuable.'

'What brings people the greatest bliss?'

'When you master the truth of life, then you are truly blissful.'

'What is the sweetest of all tastes?'

'Truth has the sweetest taste.'

'Which is the best way of life?'

'Living wisely is the best way to live.'

'When you leave this world, how can you not be sad?'

'A person who is generous, brave, moral and truthful will never feel the need to be sad.'

Alavaka was so moved by the Buddha's answers that when the king's son was sent to be sacrificed, he fell at the king's feet and begged for forgiveness. The demon became a monk and followed the Buddha till the end of his days.

Ambapali's Gift

Ambapali (also known as Amrapali) was a very beautiful woman, who was known to be rather proud of her beauty. All men, noble and ordinary, fought for her favour. One day, the Buddha came to the city of Vesali, where she lived. She heard from the locals that an ascetic had come to town. She offered the use of her mango grove to the ascetic and his followers, without the slightest idea that it was the Buddha who had arrived in Vesali.

Soon huge crowds of people began to flock to the grove. Ambapali decided to see for herself who this ascetic was that was drawing such a crowd.

When she reached the grove, the Buddha was sitting in quiet meditation beneath a tree. A golden glow seemed to surround him. Just the sight of the Buddha moved Ambapali to tears. She knew she was in the presence of a great soul. The Buddha then opened his eyes and imparted his teachings of dhamma to her. She was so overwhelmed that she invited the Buddha to a meal the next day.

When the noblemen of Vesali heard that the Buddha was to visit Ambapali, they begged her to allow them to host the Buddha instead.

'All the wealth in the kingdom will not tempt me to give away this chance to be in the Buddha's holy presence,' she said.

After serving the Buddha a simple meal that she had cooked herself, she said to him, 'O Holy One, please accept this mango grove as a gift, which your monks can use as they wish.'

The Buddha accepted her gift. And Ambapali gave up her life of luxury and vanity to become a bhikkhuni in the Buddha's order. Even today, the story of Ambapali is famous.

Jivaka, the Medicine Man

One day, a baby was found abandoned on a garbage heap, crying helplessly. Just then, Prince Abhaya, son of King Bimbisara, passed by.

When he saw the child, he was overcome with pity. He took him in and brought him up as his own son.

The boy was named Jivaka. When he grew up, his father sent him to a university, where he studied medicine. He became one of the most skilful doctors of his time.

Whenever any royal member was ill, it was Jivaka who would be called upon to attend to them. But of all his patients, the Buddha was his favourite. It was Jivaka who looked after the Buddha throughout his life. In fact, Jivaka built a monastery in his own garden and presented it to the Buddha. Soon he too converted and became a monk.

Pasenadi, the Buddha's Friend

Gautama Buddha had a lot of good friends, who remained close to him throughout his travels. King Pasenadi of Kosala was one such companion. He was also one of the first royal converts to become a bhikkhu and follow the Buddha's teachings.

Pasenadi was said to be a happy-go-lucky king, who loved the good life. Most of all, he loved his food. He had become rather overweight, when Siddhartha lectured him on the value of eating moderately. Not content to leave it at that, he taught Pasenadi's nephew a poem on the ills of

overeating and made him recite it to his uncle
every time Pasenadi sat down for a meal. Not only
did Pasenadi learn self-control, but he also lost a
lot of weight and became healthy.

When Pasenadi's wife gave birth to a daughter,
he was bitterly disappointed for he badly wanted
a son. It was his friend Gautama who explained
to him how wonderful daughters are. Later, that
same little girl became Pasenadi's favourite child.

10 Symbols in Buddhism

Buddhism has many symbols that the followers of the faith use across the world. Here are a few:

The Lotus

The lotus is a symbol of purity. According to the Buddhist texts, just as a lotus stays pure even though it grows in muddy swamps, a true follower of the Buddha must stay pure even through the murkiness of life. This is why there are many images of the Buddha sitting on a lotus flower.

The Buddha's Footprints

The footprints of the Buddha are considered to be very auspicious. There are detailed patterns imprinted on them, each of which has an important meaning.

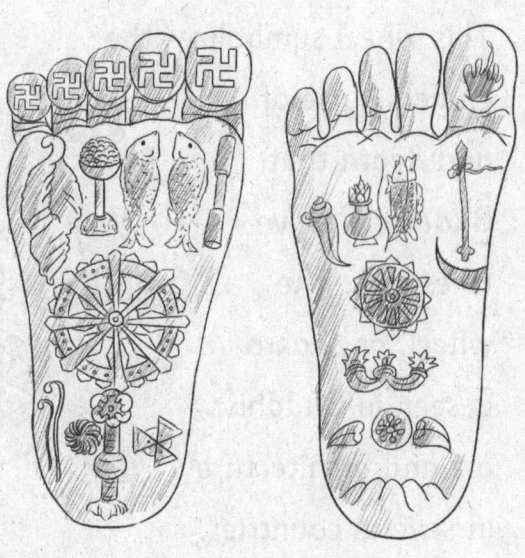

The Mandala

Mandala literally means circle, which represents the universe. The mandala aids Buddhists in their meditation.

The Dharma Wheel

This wheel symbolizes the
endless cycle of life
and death that
Buddhists strive
to escape. The
wheel, or chakra,
is seen in Buddhist
art and architecture
in several countries.

11 Timeline

The exact dates of the Buddha's birth and death were not accurately recorded. But many historical documents agree on the time period of the important events in the Buddha's life.

563 BCE   Siddhartha is born in Lumbini.

563–547 BCE   Siddhartha spends a happy childhood in Kapilavastu.

547 BCE   At the age of sixteen, Siddhartha marries Yashodhara.

542 BCE   Bimbisara becomes king of Magadha.

547–534 BCE   Siddhartha spends thirteen years in wedded bliss.

534 BCE   He sees the four sights that change his life.

534 BCE   Yashodhara gives birth to a baby boy, Rahula. That same year, Siddhartha gives up his worldly possessions and leaves home, beginning his quest.

528 BCE   Siddhartha becomes a Buddha and achieves enlightenment in Bodhgaya. That same year, he delivers his first sermon in Sarnath.

483 BCE   Gautama Buddha attains nirvana in Kusinara. That same year, the first Buddhist council is held, during which the tenets of Buddhism are fixed.

12 Bibliography

Biography. 'Buddha Biography.' https://www.biography.com/people/buddha-9230587.

Buddhanet. 'Life of the Buddha.' https://www.buddhanet.net/e-learning/buddhism/lifebuddha/index.htm.

Chowdhury, Rohini. *Gautama Buddha: The Lord of Wisdom*. Puffin Lives Series. New Delhi: Penguin Books India, 2011.

Kramer, Jacqueline. 'Yasodhara and Siddhartha: The Enlightenment of Buddha's Wife.' In *Turning Wheel* (Summer 2010) by Buddhist Peace Fellowship. http://www.bhikkhuni.net/wp-content/uploads/2014/06/yasodhara.pdf.